SCRIBNER
1230 Avenue of the Americas
New York, NY 10020

First combined edition January 2007

SCRIBNER and design are trademarks of Macmillan Library Reference USA, Inc., used under license by Simon & Schuster, the publisher of this work.

For information about special discounts for bulk purchases,
please contact Simon & Schuster Special Sales:
1-800-456-6798 or business@simonandschuster.com

Designed by Pascal Lemaître; colors by P. Lemaître and E. Phuon

Text set in Berthold Garamond

Manufactured in the United States of America

These titles were previously published individually by Scribner

10 9 8 7 6 5 4 3 2 1

Library of Congress Cataloging-in-Publication Data
Morrison, Toni.
Who's got game? : three fables / by Toni Morrison and Slade Morrison ; pictures by Pascal Lemaitre.—1st combined ed.
     p. cm.
Contents: The ant or the grasshopper?—The lion or the mouse?—Poppy or the snake?
1. Fables, American. I. Morrison, Slade. II. Lemaître, Pascal. III. Title
PS3563.O8749A6 2005
813'.54—dc22 2005051729

ISBN-13: 978-0-7432-8391-5
ISBN-10:   0-7432-8391-0

THE ANT OR
THE GRASSHOPPER?

FOXY G and his ace **KiD A** were hanging in the park.
They romped each day till the sun's last ray
and didn't stop till dark.

They climbed trees, tore up their knees,

dunked balls and shot hoops from afar.

Swam in the pool where the water was cool

and sang with their air guitars.

One hot day
as they lay in the shade
Kid A turned to his friend and said:

Got to split, Foxy. The summer's been fun.

Time to dump this place, get back in the race.
There's a lot of work to be done.

Hold on, I just thought of a tune.

Listen up, Kid. This will rocket the moon!

Foxy raised his wings, rubbed them hard,
making music so def it drew a crowd.

That's cool, Foxy G,
but listen to me.

Vacation is gone; the days getting short.
We can't hang forever on the basketball court!

Then split,
Kid A.

Who's in your way?

As for me,
Foxy G . . .

I have to let
my music
out!

Kid A did the chores and shopped the stores.

And day and night, out of sight,

Foxy's music blew clear and wild. It was so sweet with his outrageous beat.

Kid A began to dance.
　　He popped his fingers, shook his hips,
　　　　a big fat grin on his lips.

Hard at work or fast asleep,
he couldn't stop his dancing feet.

He fixed the stove, raked the leaves,
covered the shrubs so they wouldn't freeze.

He heaped and piled and baked
and stored jam
to be spread
on slices of bread.

when winter howled at the door.

Still out in the park was Foxy
where the wind began to bite.
He wanted to finish one more tune
before the coming night.
Unfolding his wings from a cardboard box,

he saw their edges crumble.

He tried to patch the delicate parts

but his fingers only fumbled.

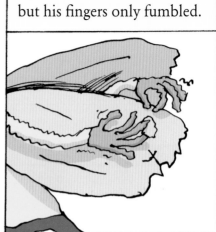

Weak with hunger and shivering cold,

he couldn't make the faintest sound.

No grooves; no moves; no blast, no rips.
No riffs or spiffs, no peaks or dips.

Battling shame, he left the park.
There was nothing else to do
but swallow his pride and drag his wings
back to the neighborhood.
Trying not to shake, to break or quake,

He knocked on Kid A's door.

I'm cold, Kid, with nothing to eat.
My wings are freezing and I'm dead on my feet.
I'm not going to make it out here with no heat.
So, say, my friend. Can I come in?

Kid A munched a doughnut and scoped his friend.

You're cold? Hungry? No place to stay?

Look at you, man.

Well, what can I say?

I planned ahead and stored up things.

You wasted time on those funky wings.

Foxy tried to smile but it didn't work.

The tears in his eyes made him feel like a jerk.

You should have known

what tomorrow would bring.

Then you wouldn't be begging for anything.

I'm an artist, that's what I do!

You loved my music so respect me, too !

Kid smirked while he said . . .

You think feeling
is better than
dealing.

But I'm standing,
not kneeling.

And my family's fed.

WHERE'S YOUR HEAD?

You sleep in a box;

I've got a bed.

But music's been good for you and me.
It ought to deserve your sympathy.

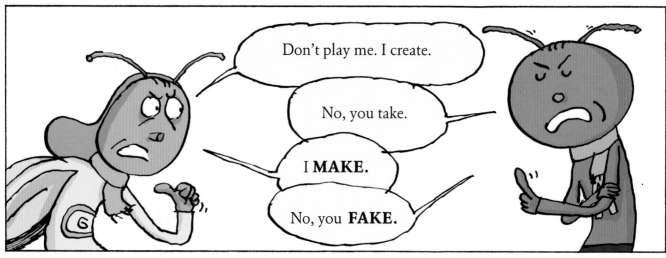

Foxy stumbled off into the night,
his head held high, his arms wrapped tight
around his wings with all his might.

THE LION OR
THE MOUSE?

to Nidal
T.M.

to Kali-Ma
S.M.

to my dad.
P.L.

Lion, strutting over the wide savannah,

raised his head and roared:

Shaking his mane, Lion ran through the tall grass.

He leaped over rocks.

He clawed the trees.

He bounded through bushes prickly with thorns.

Suddenly he yelped. Then he stumbled. Then he bumbled. Then he mumbled and fell down.

Pain sliced through one of his paws. Pain so sharp he could barely talk. In a little baby voice he whispered:

Listen up. Listen up.
No ifs, maybes, ands, or buts.
I was running over the land.
I ran like the wind and
I looked so grand.
Now I can't get a roar
from my mighty jaws
because, because a thorn
is stuck in one of my paws.
Tigers, hyenas, or elephants too,
please help me out.
I don't care who.

Tiger sauntered by and heard Lion moan.

Not me, I have to hurry home. My baby's alone. I promised to bring her an ice cream cone.

Hyena skittered by and heard Lion groan.

Not me, I have to bury a bone. I'm on my own. Besides, I'm on the telephone.

Elephant lumbered by and heard Lion weep.

Not me, I have a date to keep. A floor to sweep. And I never touch meat.

Monkey watched all the animals leave and said Who, me? to Lion's plea.

Sorry, King Lion. I heard you whine, but I'm busy right now and I don't have time.

My wife is calling.

My mother is sick.

My roof is falling.

I have fruit to pick.

Lion sighed and tried again and again to pull the thorn from his hind paw. But he could not reach it. Not with his teeth. Not with another paw. The more he tried, the deeper the thorn sank, and the sharper the pain. He had lost all hope when he heard a squeak from the bushes nearby.

His voice was almost gone, but he was able to murmur:

Listen up!

Listen up!

No ifs, maybes, ands, or buts. I am the SADDEST *in all the land.*

Mouse crept slowly toward Lion. Slowly. Slowly. Then he wrapped his tail around the tip of the thorn and pulled.

Nothing.

Next he gripped the thorn with his tiny paws.

Nothing.

Then he clenched the thorn in his teeth. And **OUT** it came.

Lion sighed with relief. Tears of gratitude moistened his eyes as he gazed at his sore and tender paw.

Smiling and happy, they parted company.
Lion limped back to his den to recover.
Mouse scampered back to his nest hole in the bushes.

The next day Mouse woke feeling very strange.
His heart sounded like a drum in his chest.

His teeth felt as sharp as razors.

When he poked his head out of his nest and yawned, out came a powerful roar.

He fluffed up the fur around his neck to make it look like a mane . . .

. . . and, flashing his teeth, ran into the tall grass.

He attacked the trees, leaped over rocks, roaring at other animals.

LISTEN UP!
LISTEN UP!

NO IFS, MAYBES, ANDS, OR BUTS.
I'M THE RULER OF THE WORLD!
MY TEETH ARE SHARP;
MY MANE IS CURLED.
MY TAIL IS A WHIP;
MY PAWS ARE STEEL.
MY MUSCLES RIP;
MY POWER IS REAL.
I CAN EAT YOU UP FOR
MY EVENING MEAL.
My

Tiger, Hyena, and Elephant heard only a squeak coming from Mouse. Monkey wondered what made the fur around Mouse's neck stick out like spikes. He began to laugh. Tiger joined in, and then Hyena and Elephant. They all stared at Mouse and every time he squeaked or fluffed his fur, they laughed harder.

ngry and frustrated, Mouse ran to Lion's den, shouting,

Lion rose up and ambled to the door. He was ashamed of being saved by a weak little mouse, and was hiding in his den. Now he wanted to tell Mouse to go away but he could not break his word.

So he listened to his new friend whining, complaining.

Day after day after day after day Mouse knocked on Lion's door to tell how and why the animals were laughing at him.

It must be the mane, I think.

It's not as long as yours.

Maybe its my tongue; it's pink.

Not wide and red like yours.

It could be my paws that stink.

They're not as big as yours.

So Lion fashioned a mane from
his own fur and gave it to Mouse.

Then he cut from red velvet
a wide tongue for Mouse
to put in his jaws.

Next he made four big boots
to look like paws for Mouse to wear.

Nothing helped. Each time that Mouse appeared with a new contraption, the animals laughed even harder.

Finally, after much thinking, Mouse had an idea.

He ran to Lion . . .

. . . and said:

What I need is a proper throne.
I'll have to make your den my home.

I won't let them see me anymore.
Laughter can't reach behind your door.

Lion was angry, but so pleased to be away from the pestering mouse. He left his den and moved to a hill overlooking his former home.

You can hear this day
nearby and far away
Mouse squeaking
the whole day long . . .

. . . and Lion singing
a wiser song:

POPPY OR
THE SNAKE?

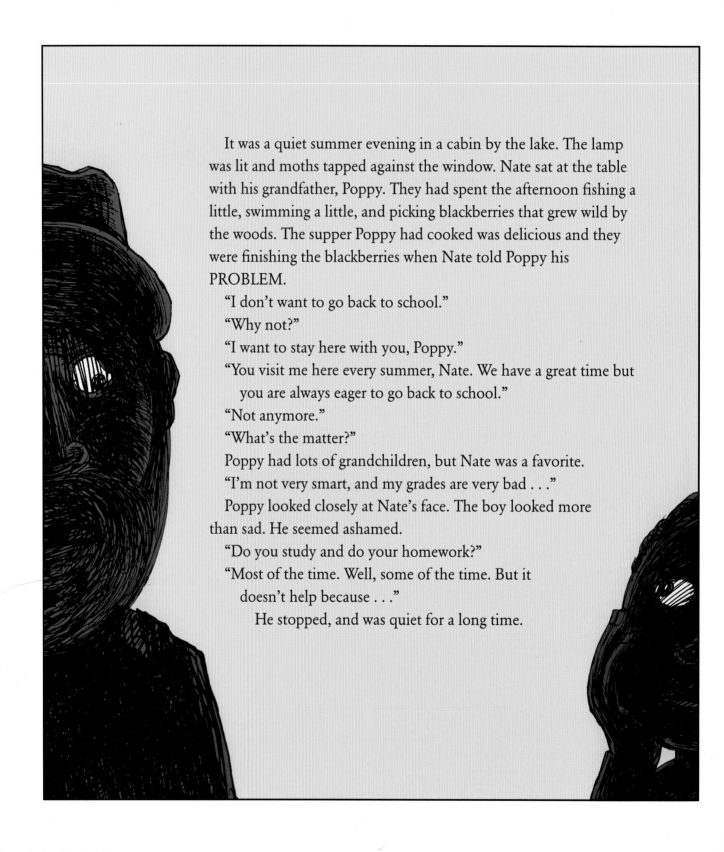

It was a quiet summer evening in a cabin by the lake. The lamp was lit and moths tapped against the window. Nate sat at the table with his grandfather, Poppy. They had spent the afternoon fishing a little, swimming a little, and picking blackberries that grew wild by the woods. The supper Poppy had cooked was delicious and they were finishing the blackberries when Nate told Poppy his PROBLEM.

"I don't want to go back to school."

"Why not?"

"I want to stay here with you, Poppy."

"You visit me here every summer, Nate. We have a great time but you are always eager to go back to school."

"Not anymore."

"What's the matter?"

Poppy had lots of grandchildren, but Nate was a favorite.

"I'm not very smart, and my grades are very bad . . ."

Poppy looked closely at Nate's face. The boy looked more than sad. He seemed ashamed.

"Do you study and do your homework?"

"Most of the time. Well, some of the time. But it doesn't help because . . ."

He stopped, and was quiet for a long time.

"Come on, you can tell me."

"Dad says I'm lazy. Mom says I don't concentrate."

"Which is it?"

"Both, I guess. I sit at my desk, but I can't seem to pay
attention. There's so much going on that's more fun than
schoolwork."

"I see."

Poppy thought awhile and then got up and went to the
closet. He took out a pair of shiny boots. When he put them
on, Nate asked, "Are you going out?"

"No. These are my remembering boots. They
help me remember what I don't want to forget."

"How do they work?"

"Well, right now they're helping me
remember that paying attention is just a way of
taking yourself seriously."

"I don't understand."

Poppy cleared the dishes from the table. Then he
turned down the lamp. When he sat down, both of
their faces shone in the moonlight that flooded
the room.

I drove out to the pier to fish one evening.

The weather was cool, and the fish were hungry. I caught several before it got too dark to see.

So I packed my gear and headed for my truck. When I got there, I saw something caught under one of my tires. I reached down to pull it loose and discovered it wasn't a branch or a vine . . .

. . . but a SNAKE.

I must have rolled over it when I parked.
I took out my flashlight and pointed it toward the snake.

SUDDENLY, its eyes opened and its tail flicked. It scared me, so I shouted.

WHOA!

The snake didn't move again, but when I leaned down to get a closer look,
IT SPOKE...

Well, let me see
  if I can help.
If you'll be very still
I think I can move my truck.

THAT'S MORE LIKE IT! GET A MOVE ON, WILL YOU!

I hesitated.

NOW WHAT'S THE MATTER?

Well, you are a SNAKE and a **POISONOUS** one too.

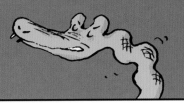

STILL.

You might change
your mind.

I know plenty
folk who do.

I changed
my own mind
once in a while.

*You messing
with me,
ain't you?
You making
stuff up
so you don't
have to help
me.*

got into the truck and started the engine. Slowly, I let the truck ease forward.

The snake slid around a little to make sure all of him was together.
He crawled close to the truck door, raised up, and opened his mouth.

Beautiful, dude.

BEAUTIFUL.

I'm glad it worked. I'll be off now.

OFF? OFF **WHERE?**

HOME

I should have known you was a clown. **I** have to promise to be good, but **you** can drive on off. NEVER MIND WHAT YOU DONE.

I did what we agreed. What more do you want?

He slithered closer to my window.

I been pinned under your tire for hours. In pain, starving, scared out of my mind. And you mean to tell me you not going to take me home and give me something to eat?

I thought about it and decided the snake meant what he said.
There was no reason for him to bite a friend. So I picked him up and put him in the bed of the truck.

When we got to the cabin I filled a bowl with milk for him. Snake sipped until

it was all gone, and then, yawning, he curled up and went to sleep.

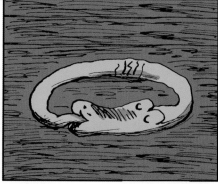

The next morning, at breakfast, I noticed Snake had bruises where the tire had struck him. Some of his scales had fallen off, and there were tiny scratches too. I got some medicine and woke him.

After a meal of toast and milk, Snake asked if he could stay another night. I had to smile. He had a sassy mouth, but he seemed like a good soul underneath.

After all, he'd sworn he wouldn't bite me, RIGHT?

thought about that while I drove into the village.

I was late getting back, and when I opened the door, Snake . . .

And we mean what we say, don't we?

OH, MAN, WE DOWN. YOU KNOW. DOWN.

I made supper and we talked about this and that.

The days passed peacefully until I noticed that Snake seemed bored, restless.

Why don't you get you a TV? Liven this place up.

I like the peace and quiet.

Not even a radio? You don't want no radio?

NO.

Don't you get lonesome?

NO.

I like my own company.

Is that right?

Snake yawned and curled up on the mat near the stove.

I wasn't sleepy, so I sat on the porch and watched the stars for a while.

 When I came back in, I noticed snake had slithered closer
to my bed to sleep. Early the next morning before
the sun had risen . . .

Snake flicked his stringy, forked tongue, saying as casually as you please,

HEY, MAN. I'M A
SNAKE.

Poppy looked at Nate and laughed, slapping his knees. Nate stared at his grandfather. "What happened? You mean he bit you and you didn't die?"

"He bit me, all right. And no, I didn't die. You see, I thought about what snake had promised me. He said he wouldn't even think of biting me. He never said he wouldn't bite me—just that he wouldn't think of it. So I took a precaution and on the day I went to the village, I got a snake serum."

"Oh, that's what saved you!" Nate grinned.

"Not entirely. Paying attention is what saved me. And I never want to forget that, so I figured out a way to remember it."

Poppy turned up the lamp. He lifted his legs and stretched them out on the table.

Then, in the glow, Nate saw his
grandfather's remembering boots.
They were beautiful and made
of the softest, shiniest snakeskin.

TONI MORRISON

SLADE MORRISON

PASCAL LEMAÎTRE

TONI MORRISON, who is best known for her fiction, teaches at Princeton University. Her novels include *Song of Solomon* (1977), *Beloved* (1987), *Jazz* (1992), *Paradise* (1998), and *Love* (2003).

SLADE MORRISON has coauthored two previous books with Toni Morrison. A painter by profession, he has a home and studio in Rockland County, New York.

PASCAL LEMAÎTRE has been a freelance illustrator since 1990. He illustrated *Supercat* and worked with the Morrisons on a children's book, *The Book of Mean People*.

Photographs by Timothy Greenfield-Sanders